The Grand House & The Great Diaper Shortage

Therese M. Quigley

Illustrated by Aja Pragana

Therese Quigley

Visit our website at
www.StillwaterPress.com
for more information.

First Stillwater River Publications Edition

Library of Congress Control Number: 2020916825

ISBN: 978-1-952521-45-4

1 2 3 4 5 6 7 8 9 10
Written by Therese M. Quigley
Illustrated by Aja Pragana
Published by Stillwater River Publications,
Pawtucket, RI, USA.

Publisher's Cataloging-In-Publication Data
(Prepared by The Donohue Group, Inc.)

Names: Quigley, Therese M., author. | Pragana, Aja, illustrator.
Title: The grand house / Therese M. Quigley ; illustrated by Aja Pragana.
Description: First Stillwater River Publications edition. | Pawtucket, RI, USA :
Stillwater River Publications, [2020] | Interest age level: 008-012. |
Summary: "Told from the perspective of the house, 'The Grand House' tells
the story of the families, children, dogs and even a shop that existed within
its walls"--Provided by publisher.
Identifiers: ISBN 9781952521454
Subjects: LCSH: Dwellings--New England--History--Juvenile fiction. |
Dwellings--Conservation and restoration--New England--Juvenile fiction. |
Architecture--New England--Juvenile fiction. |
CYAC: Dwellings--New England--History--Fiction. |
Dwellings--Conservation and restoration--New England--Fiction. |
Architecture--New England--Fiction.
Classification: LCC PZ7.1.Q458 Gr 2020 | DDC [Fic]--dc23

TEXT SET IN BRIOSO

*The views and opinions expressed
in this book are solely those of the author
and do not necessarily reflect the views
and opinions of the publisher.*

I dedicate this book to my husband,
Bob, who has never complained about the time
and money I spend on my sewing projects and
classes, but instead, encourages me.

Also to Peter, Sara, and Liam.
I love you all.
You give meaning to my life!

—T.Q.

Inspiration

This story was inspired by my friend, Amy, of Amy's Fabric Treasures, who lovingly restored an old house that had been, by turns, much loved and much neglected. To the delight of her many customers and students, she relocated her shop to the restored house and re-opened her business in Westport, Massachusetts in February of 2020.

Thank you, Amy, for your kindness and good cheer, your remarkable patience, your encyclopedic knowledge of sewing and textiles, and your commitment to the environment by consigning fabric treasures.

Thank you also to Ryan for putting the whole adventure in motion!

The Grand House

Do you know that every house has a story? For example, people used to call me The Grand House, but now I am The Treasure House. This is how it happened.

Mr. Edwin Small and Mrs. Enid Small built me for their very large family: Elizabeth, Elsa, Emma, Eddie, Ezra, Ernest and their little dog, Puff.

"We are not big people," Mr. Small said to his wife, "but I would like a big house, a GRAND house, and I will build it on Grand Avenue." Mr. Small was a house builder, a very GOOD house builder, and so he built a very grand house, indeed. I have five bedrooms, three bathrooms, a large kitchen and dining room, two living rooms, a library and a very grand porch.

Mr. Small built many houses, but I am the only one he LOVES. He made my porch so big that the whole family could gather to admire the Milky Way at night, or watch the dew rise early on a summer morning. They could eat picnics in my shade on hot summer days and sleep in my hammocks at night, enjoying the cool country breezes.

They celebrated snowy nights in front of my fireplace, decorated with winter greens and berries. On those nights, they fired up the hand-crafted brick oven in my toasty kitchen to make their own family-size pizzas and flavored popcorn! Oh, the aromas that filled my rooms then!

Mr. and Mrs. Small and their children took very good care of me. They polished my floors and windows. They shined my wood and cleaned my mirrors. They swept my closets and put the trash outside. My bathrooms always smelled fresh, my beds always looked neat, my lights always shone brightly, and my kitchen was spotless. The family was so proud of me, their very own GRAND house!

Puff's doghouse sparkled, too!

One day, as Mr. Small was looking out his window and watching his little dog go in and out of his little doghouse, he said to Mrs. Small, "Now that Elizabeth, Elsa, Emma, Eddie, Ezra and Ernest are all grown up, we don't need this grand house anymore. Look at how happy Puff is in his TINY house. That's all we need! I would like a tiny house! On wheels!"

6

So Mr. Small, the house builder, built a TINY house on wheels for himself and Mrs. Small, and several others for his grown-up children. "It's time for another family to live in this very grand house and ENJOY it as much as we did," he said.

The new renters were Mr. and Mrs. Popper, their children, Vince and Vance, and their little dog, Cooper. (They called him Cooper the Pooper!) Mr. and Mrs. Popper didn't see that I was grand. They let Vince and Vance write on my walls and put sticky candy on my windows. They didn't polish my woodwork, or shine my floors, or clean my kitchen, or put out the trash. They broke my railing and spilled paint on my porch. Then Vince made a leak in the bathroom and Vance poked a hole in the basement wall. But Mr. and Mrs. Popper were too busy to see, and soon a mouse family moved in. The mice made a mess in the kitchen, and then Cooper the Pooper... Yes! He made a mess, too!

I was very sad. I didn't feel grand. I didn't smell grand. And I didn't look grand! When Mr. Small saw how sad I was, he told the Popper family to leave, and he sold me to a lady named Polly. Polly and her husband Pete, and their son Pickle, had GREAT plans for me!

Polly had collected many beautiful treasures, but she couldn't see them all because they were packed into a very small space. She wanted to restore my beauty and display her treasures in my lovely rooms! Polly said, "This house will become a grand gathering place for friends who will turn my treasures into new and useful things. They will learn crafts, embroidery, sewing, knitting, quilting, and all their supplies will be right here!" Can you imagine how excited I was to hear that?

Polly and her friends cleaned and polished and painted, while Pete and Pickle fixed leaks and holes and broken lights, and made shelves for all the lovely rooms to hold all the treasures: colorful fabric, trims, threads, laces, patterns, buttons, zippers and more. They even painted fancy lettering over my fireplace, while soups and stews were simmering on my stove!

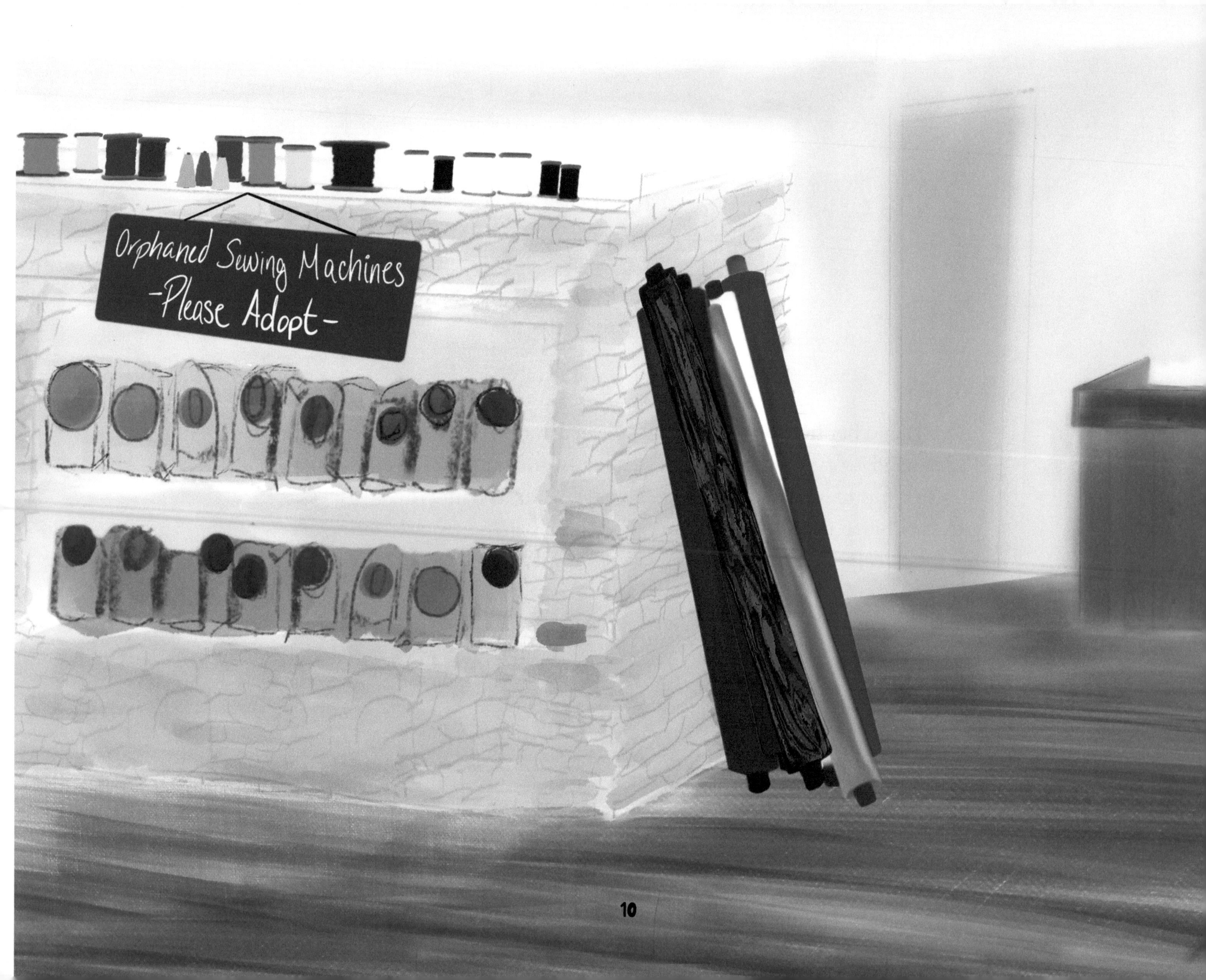
Orphaned Sewing Machines
-Please Adopt-

Soon I was glowing! I smelled good! I looked good! And the people who came to shop and learn felt good! They said, "What a beautiful house!"

"What lovely rooms!"

"What perfect colors!"

"So relaxing!"

"I'm never leaving!"

Polly is happy to spend her days teaching and sewing in such a GRAND house! And although Pete is not a house builder like Mr. Small, he built garages in the back, and that's where he and Pickle keep their car collection. Some of Polly's customers bring picnic lunches to eat on the lawn, and others admire the cars. Sometimes I hear those old cars purring as I close my eyes at night!

Early one morning, I heard many tires turning into my driveway, and do you know who it was? Mr. Small and his family had come to see me! They were driving their tiny houses on wheels! They all lined up in my driveway, then hopped out and stared at me! Mr. Small put his hands on his hips, leaned back, and looked at me for a long time. Finally, he said, "I love this Grand House." And Polly answered, "Me, too. It's a Treasure!"

What makes a house grand?

It's whatever makes you say WOW! It might be a wrap-around porch or deck, or a huge finished basement. It might be cozy rooms with fireplaces, or large, airy rooms with big, sunny windows. It might be built-in shelving and window seats. Or maybe it's stained glass, fancy trim, and turrets. Or French doors, pocket doors, or eye-catching staircases. Or is it the memories you make there?

Here is a small sample of popular house styles in New England.

FEDERAL

DUTCH COLONIAL

CAPE COD

GREEK REVIVAL

COLONIAL

VICTORIAN

New England House Styles

15

The Great Diaper Shortage

About nine months after Polly filled her grand house with fabric treasures and opened her shop to friends and customers, a baby boom occurred. Babies were being born all over town, and suddenly Mr. and Mrs. Small had six grandbabies! Each of their six grown-up children welcomed a new baby into the family, and several neighbors had twins. Even Puff had a puppy!

Soon, Big Foods Market ran out of baby food, so the train started bringing extra boxes of rice cereal, baby yogurt, baby formula and baby bottles. The puréed fruits and vegetables sold so fast that new parents started planting berries, squash, and spinach in their backyards.

To make matters worse, there was a diaper shortage! At first, helicopters brought some in from other towns and dropped them, fluttering, over the houses that needed them. But soon there were no more diapers to be found anywhere! The factories couldn't make them fast enough! That's when people started making their own. Soon the stores ran out of supplies to make reusable diapers and diaper covers, but not Polly! She seemed to have an endless supply of fabric, elastic, pins, thread and sewing machines, collected over many years.

Parents came from miles away, some with babies in backpacks or strollers, to buy supplies from Polly. They would call ahead and she would meet them on the porch to hand over everything they needed to make diapers at home. Or they would telephone and she would mail the supplies to them. Polly went to the post office three times a

week to make sure every baby in need of diapers got the supplies that only she could provide. You see, other fabric stores had run out of the needed materials.

Whenever Polly's supplies got low, she simply went into the basement of her clean, fresh-smelling grand house with its rows and rows of buttons, zippers, trims, scissors, needles and fabrics of all kinds, including diaper fabric. She brought it all upstairs with her and continued providing an "essential service" to her community.

Then the zoo called. They had an injured chimpanzee who needed diapers. They heard that Polly could help! Polly asked Pickle's grandma to make some diapers for the zookeepers, which she did. She made the diaper covers in red and white checked fabric.

The animal shelter called next. They had a dog named Gigi who needed diapers, so Pickle's grandma made doggie diapers, too.

The diaper covers were made of beagle and bone fabric.

She also made diapers for Farmer Eliot's duck, Lemon, who was born unable to walk. Pickle's grandma chose blue fabric with yellow rubber ducks on it. She loved picking just the right fabric for each customer, and she loved helping Polly provide what people (and animals) needed.

After about six months, Polly and Pickle's grandma were looking forward to the babies outgrowing their need for diapers. They wanted Polly's customers to meet at the Grand House for classes. They wanted her students to have another fashion show. They wanted their lives to go back to 'normal.' Then Pickle got an idea to remind people that his mom's business offered a lot more than just diaper fabric!

Pickle's dad had been teaching him to drive. Every Saturday, they took one of the old cars out to drive around town, so Pickle decided to advertise his mother's house of fabric treasures while driving.

He asked his dad, "Which car should I use? The glossy yellow one is my favorite, but the lime green one is the newest. The baby blue one is perfect for the baby boom, and then there's your favorite, the red one."

"Use the red one. It will attract the most attention," his dad suggested. So Pickle offered free rides in a basket attached to a kite pulled by his dad's old red car! And Pickle drove!

"First I need to practice," Pickle thought. So he took Puff and her baby, Pup, and put them in the basket with a soft blue blanket. Then he attached the basket to a shiny, red kite with a long, waving tail. Then he tied the tail to the red car.

As Pickle drove, the kite rose up, up into the sky, and with it the basket with his doggie passengers. Pickle was so excited! His idea worked! But then, the basket began to tip, and little Pup's nose peeped over the edge. Then little Pup's ears appeared, then his eyes, and suddenly his whole body was tipping out of the basket and sliding down the kite string!

Puff jumped into action. She grabbed her puppy's tail between her teeth and started hauling Pup back into the basket. A crowd was gathering below. "Stop! Stop," they shouted to Pickle. "Your cargo is tipping!"

One man in the crowd was a worker at the Cape Cod Marine Life Center. He had just purchased a new fish net for work. As he looked up, Puff slipped out of the basket and started tumbling through the air with Pup's tail in her teeth. "I've got you," he shouted, holding the net up and running to catch the falling dogs. The crowd stopped and stared in amazement as the man lifted his net and Puff and Pup dropped safely in!

Someone from the crowd took pictures and sent them to the newspaper with details about Pickle's efforts to advertise his mother's shop, and the man who rescued Puff and Pup. "We have enough advertising now," Polly told Pickles. "We don't need any more," Pickles agreed.

"I think I'll leave Puff and Pup home the next time I fly a kite from the car," he told her. Polly laughed and went back to her Treasure House.

WHAT REALLY HAPPENED—Amy's Fabric Treasures and the Pandemic of 2020

Four weeks after the grand opening of Amy's Fabric Treasures in Westport, Massachusetts, the COVID-19 pandemic (not diaper shortage) hit the United States, and the demand for face masks (not diapers) sky-rocketed. Out of necessity, the Center for Disease Control issued instructions for DIY face masks, and people started making them at home; a cottage industry was born. While many other businesses were forced to close, some temporarily and others permanently, Amy's newly-relocated business was as busy as ever because it had the materials everyone needed.

Schools, colleges, and childcare centers closed, forcing parents to stay home from work to care for their children and help them with online school assignments. Adults who were able to work from home, instead of the office, did so. Many predicted a baby boom in nine months.

In the first twelve weeks of the pandemic, Amy sold over 5,000 yards of quarter-inch elastic, in addition to cotton fabrics for face coverings. When it seemed she had finally run out of elastic, she searched through the consigned materials stored in the basement and found more! She was able to continue supplying customers near and far with materials to make essential PPE (personal protective equipment) long after other suppliers' stocks were depleted.

Amy provided both drive-up and mail order services, going to the Post Office three times a week. And her mother, an accomplished seamstress of many years, made fabric face masks from her home to sell to customers as far away as Florida.

Congratulations to Amy's Fabric Treasures for staying afloat and for filling a need during the Pandemic of 2020!

If you are interested in learning how to restore an old house, consult these online sources:

www.OldHouseOnline.com

www.CountryLiving.com

www.TheCraftsmanBlog.com

If you would like to learn more about tiny houses, I invite you to do some research at the following websites:

www.TinyHomeBuilders.com

www.TheSpruce.com

www.CountryLiving.com

If you would like to build a doghouse, do some research first. Check out the following articles online:

16 Free DIY Dog House Plans, by Stacy Fisher 3/26/20 at www.TheSprucePets.com

Bring the Luck Home: 16 Pallet Dog House at www.Palletlist.com or www.Pinterest.com / 10 Architects

Create Stylish Doghouses for a good cause, by Hadley Keller 7/30/18 at www.ArchitecturalDigest.com

If you want to learn more about American house styles, check out the following book. Parts 2 and 3 are especially helpful. *Under Every Roof, a Kid's Style and Field Guide to the Architecture of American Houses,* c. 1993, by Patricia Brown Glenn, illustrated by Joe Stites.

To discover and to admire some really OLD houses, look at www.ForTheLoveOfOldHouses.com

Making a gift to your community

Are you looking for a service project that you can do alone or with friends? Take pictures of the oldest or most interesting houses in your neighborhood or town. Put them into an album and label each one with its address and the year it was built. You can search for the address online, and the real estate listing should pop up. This will tell you the year the house was built and even the style of architecture! If you need better information, you can search for the addresses at your Town Hall.

Once your album is complete, sign it and date it. Give it a title. Then donate it to your public library or your local historical society. (You can also make your album available online!)

CPSIA information can be obtained
at www.ICGtesting.com
Printed in the USA
BVHW092056031120
592456BV00001B/4